This book
belongs to...

Time for a Tale

a collection of Nursery and Fairy stories

retold by Lucy Kincaid

Illustrated by

Elisabeth Woodhouse

and Gerry Embleton

BRIMAX BOOKS

Published by
BRIMAX BOOKS, CAMBRIDGE, ENGLAND
First Published 1975 — Third impression 1977

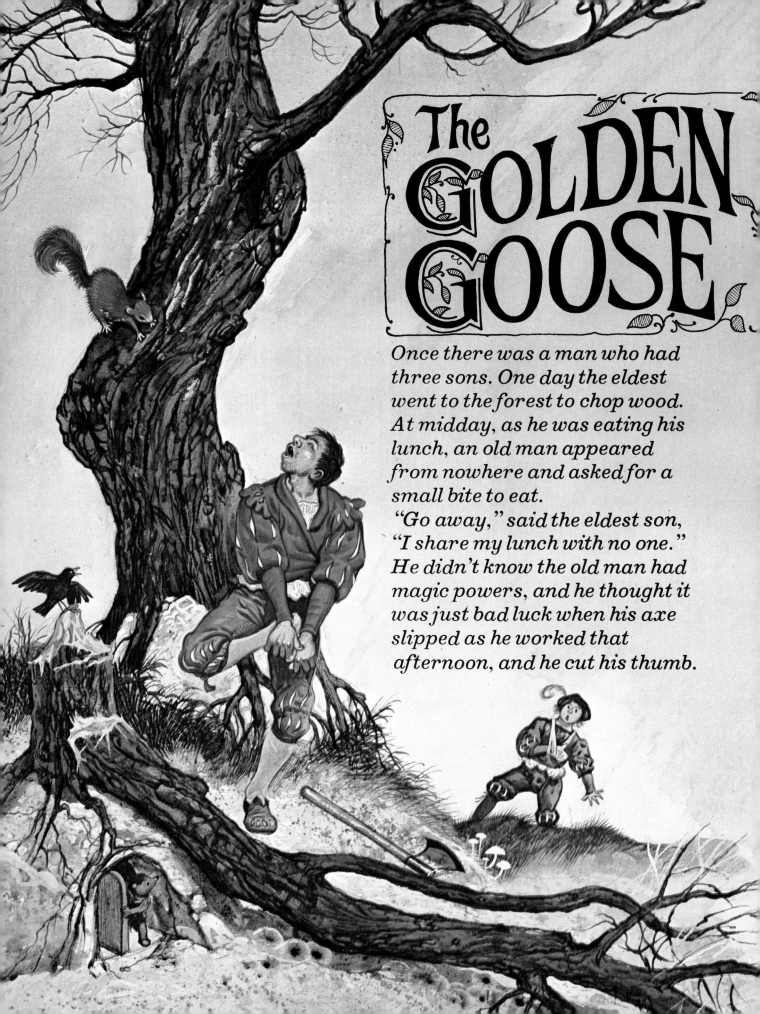

The GOLDEN GOOSE

Once there was a man who had three sons. One day the eldest went to the forest to chop wood. At midday, as he was eating his lunch, an old man appeared from nowhere and asked for a small bite to eat.

"Go away," said the eldest son, "I share my lunch with no one." He didn't know the old man had magic powers, and he thought it was just bad luck when his axe slipped as he worked that afternoon, and he cut his thumb.

The following day the middle son went to the forest. At midday the old man appeared again. The middle son was as greedy and as ill mannered as his elder brother.

"Go away," he said, "I share my lunch with no one." He too thought it was just bad luck when a log fell on his toe and bruised it so badly that he limped all the way home.

On the third day it was the turn of the third and youngest son to go to the forest to chop wood. At midday, as the youngest son, who was called Dummling, sat eating his lunch the old man appeared yet again, and once more asked for a small bite to eat.

"Come and sit beside me," said Dummling. "What is mine is yours also. Eat your fill."

When the old man had finished every scrap of Dummling's lunch he pointed to an old and rotting tree stump.

"Cut that down," he said, "And you will find a reward for having a kind heart." And with that, he disappeared as mysteriously as he had arrived.

Dummling was curious, and though the tree was too old and rotten to be of any use to a wood-cutter, he chopped it down as the old man had suggested. Lying unharmed at the base of the stump, on a bed of dried leaves, was a goose with golden feathers. It let Dummling stroke its head, and nestled quietly in his arms when he picked it up.

"I can't leave you here," said Dummling. "Someone is sure to kill you for the sake of your golden feathers. I think I had better take you with me."

Dummling was a long way from home and he decided to spend the night at an inn. The landlord of the inn had three daughters. One of them looked enviously at the goose's golden feathers and made up her mind to have one. That night as Dummling lay asleep, she tried to pluck a feather from the goose's back. She touched the goose very gently, she didn't want it to make a noise and wake Dummling, but as she grasped the feather and tried to pull it she found to her dismay that her hand would not move.

She tried to let go of the feather and found that she couldn't.
"Oh . . . oh . . ." she cried softly, "My hand is stuck fast . . . Sister,
please pull me away."
Her sister came to help her, but as soon as she touched her dress she
found that she was stuck too. The same thing happened to the third
sister when she tried to pull the second sister free.
Dummling had decided to see something of the world before he went
home, and the next day he set off across country with the golden goose
tucked safely under his arm. He did not seem to notice the three
sisters trailing awkwardly behind him like a broken daisy chain.
He didn't seem to notice either when a disapproving clergyman tried
to pull the girls away and was caught himself. Or the clergyman's
young assistant who could not let go of the clergyman's coat tails. Or
for that matter the three diggers who were going home to lunch when
they joined in the game, and discovered too late that it wasn't a game
at all. Or, if Dummling did notice, he pretended not to.

He had heard of a King whose daughter had been promised in marriage to anyone who could make her smile.

When the sad Princess saw Dummling with his golden goose tucked under his arm and all the people tagging along behind, the first one stuck to the goose and the rest stuck to one another as if by magic (which they were of course), and all tripping over one another's heels and bumping into one another's elbows, she not only smiled, she laughed until she cried, as did everyone else who saw that strange procession.

Dummling and the Princess were married, and lived happily ever after. No one knows what happened to the golden goose and the people who were stuck to it. Maybe the magic wore off. Maybe it didn't. Maybe they are wandering still.

The End.

Jack and the BEANSTALK

Jack lived with his mother in a tumble down house. They were so poor they never seemed to have enough to eat, and one day, Jack's mother said,
"Jack, you must take the cow to market and sell her."
"If I do that we will have no milk," said Jack.
"If we don't sell her we will soon have nothing to eat at all," replied his mother.
And so, very sadly, Jack led the cow to market. He was about half way there when he met an old man.
"Is your cow for sale?" asked the old man. Jack said that she was.
"Then I'll give you five beans for her," said the old man.
Jack laughed.
"You can't buy a cow with five beans," he said.
  "Ah," said the old man, "But these are magic beans. You will make a fortune with them."
Jack couldn't resist such a good bargain. He gave the cow an affectionate pat, handed her halter to the old man, and took the five beans in exchange.

Jack's mother was furious.
"We needed money to buy food,"
she scolded. "How could you be
so stupid?" She snatched the
beans from Jack's hand and
tossed them out of the window.
"That's what I think of your
bargain," she said.
Jack went sadly to bed, without
any supper. He supposed he had
been rather silly. He would have
to go in search of work the
following day for he couldn't let
his mother starve.
Next morning he woke up bright
and early. Instead of the bright
rays of sunlight which usually
lay across his bedroom floor,
there was a large shadow. He
went to the window to see what
was blocking out the sun.
Growing from the ground below
his window was the biggest
beanstalk in the world. It
reached up . . . up . . . up into the
sky and the top of it was lost
among the clouds.
"The old man was right, they
were magic beans," he said, "I'm
going to climb to the top to see
what I can find."
Jack's mother begged him not to
go, but Jack had made up his
mind.
He climbed and climbed, up and

up. He climbed through white swirling clouds until he came to the very tip of the beanstalk, and from the top of the beanstalk he stepped into another land. It was a land just like his own except that everything in it was twice and three times as big. All the climbing had made him hungry, so he went to the door of the only house he could see and knocked boldly.

The door was opened by a huge woman. She was so big she was surely the wife of a giant.

Jack persuaded her to give him some breakfast. He had just finished eating when he heard footsteps as heavy as falling boulders and then a voice as loud as thunder.

"FEE FI FO FUM, I SMELL THE BLOOD OF AN ENGLISHMAN!"

Quick as a flash, the giant woman bundled Jack into the oven.

"Sh . . . be very, very, quiet," she said, "That's my husband. He eats boys like you for breakfast."

The huge woman, who was indeed the wife of a giant, told her husband he was mistaken and put a bowl of porridge on the table.

When he had eaten, the giant
called for his hen.
"Lay!" he ordered. And the hen
lay a golden egg.
Jack, who could see everything
that was happening through a
crack in the oven door,
determined to have that hen for
himself.

Presently the giant's head began to nod. Soon he was asleep. As quick as a bee about to sting, Jack left the oven, picked up the hen, ran to the top of the beanstalk and climbed down to earth again.

"Mother, we are going to be rich," he said.
A few days later he decided to pay another visit to the Land of Giants. His mother begged him not to go again, but he was determined.
This time he crept secretly into the big house and hid. He waited for the giant to come home. Presently he heard footsteps as heavy as falling boulders and a voice as loud as thunder.
"FEE FI FO FUM, I SMELL THE BLOOD OF AN ENGLISHMAN!"
"I'll help you look for him," said the giant's wife. "If it's the boy who stole our little hen you shall have him for breakfast."
But Jack had hidden himself well, and in the end they had to give up looking.
After breakfast the giant called for his magic harp.
"Sing!" ordered the giant. And the harp sang sweetly.
Presently the giant's head began to nod. Soon he was asleep. Jack jumped from his hiding place, snatched up the magic harp, and started to run.

"Master! Master!" called the magic harp.

The giant woke with such a roar that the people in the land below the beanstalk thought the sky was falling in.

"FEE FI FO FUM . . ." he bellowed. "I <u>DO</u> SMELL THE BLOOD OF AN ENGLISHMAN . . ."

He ran after Jack with great lumbering, thundering steps. Jack was small and nimble, and had had a good start. When he reached the top of the beanstalk he tucked the harp inside his shirt and began to climb down.

The beanstalk began to shake, and creak, and groan, as the angry giant followed him . . .

Faster went Jack . . . faster . . . and faster . . .

"Mother! . . ." he called as he neared the bottom. "Bring me an axe . . . quickly . . ."

He jumped to the ground and took the axe. He swung his arms as though he were the strongest man in the world, and with three hefty cuts the beanstalk came tumbling to the ground. There was a terrible roar as the giant fell. He made a hole so big, when he hit the ground, that both he and the beanstalk disappeared into it, and were lost forever.

As for Jack and his mother . . . well, they lived happily ever after with the hen who laid golden eggs, and the harp which sang beautiful songs. They were never poor again.

The End

Snow White and the Seven Dwarfs

Once there was a little princess whose skin was white as snow, whose cheeks were red as roses, and whose hair was black as ebony. Her name was Snow White.

She had a stepmother who was beautiful and very vain. Every day she would look into her magic mirror and ask:—

"Mirror, mirror, on the wall, who is the fairest of us all?"

The mirror always answered that the Queen was, until one fateful day, when it replied,

"Thou Queen art fair and beauteous to see,
But Snow White is fairer far than thee."

The Queen was so angry she called a servant and ordered him to take Snow White to the forest, and kill her.

The servant loved Snow White. He could not kill her, but when he returned from the forest he told the Queen he had obeyed her order, for he knew she would send someone else to do the deed if she knew Snow White was still alive.

Snow White wandered alone through the forest until she came to a small cottage. Inside, everything was arranged in sevens. She was so hungry she couldn't resist taking a small bite from each of the seven pieces of bread set upon seven plates on the wooden table.

And then, because she was tired, she lay on one of the seven beds and fell asleep. She was found by the seven dwarfs, who owned the cottage, when they returned from a day's digging at the mines.

They took pity on Snow White when she told them her story and said she could stay with them. The following day, the wicked Queen asked her magic mirror who was the fairest in the land.
"Queen, thou art of beauty rare," it replied,
"But Snow White living in the glen
With the seven little men,
Is a thousand times more fair."
The Queen was very angry because she knew her servant had deceived her. She quickly dressed herself as a pedlar and went to the dwarfs' cottage.

"Will you buy a pretty petticoat, child?" she asked Snow White, who alas, did not recognize her. The wicked Queen slipped the petticoat over Snow White's head and pulled the tapes so tightly round her waist that Snow White stopped breathing. The dwarfs found her lying on the floor when they got home. At first they thought she was dead, but when they saw the tight lace they guessed what had happened and loosened it, and Snow White began to breathe again.

The Queen thought she had killed Snow White.

When the magic mirror said that Snow White was still the fairest in the land she turned white with rage. She dressed herself in a different disguise and hastened to the dwarfs' cottage with a poisoned comb in her pedlar's basket. It was so pretty that Snow White could not resist trying it in her hair. The instant it touched her head she fell to the floor.

When the dwarfs came home they took the comb from her hair and revived her.

"You must not speak to anyone." they said. "The wicked Queen is trying to kill you."

When the magic mirror told the Queen that Snow White was still the fairest in the land she determined to kill her or die herself in the attempt. This time she took a poisoned apple to the cottage.

Alas, Snow White forgot the dwarf's warning, and took a bite from the apple.

This time, the dwarfs could not revive her.

This time, the magic mirror replied to the Queen:—

"Thou Queen are the fairest in all the land."

The dwarfs laid Snow White in a crystal case in a forest glade, and kept watch over her day and night, for they had grown to love her. One day a Prince came riding by. When he saw Snow White, whose skin was still as white as snow, whose cheeks were still as red as roses, whose hair was still as black as ebony, he pleaded with the dwarfs to let him take her home to his palace. The Prince looked so sad when they refused that the dwarfs changed their minds, and agreed to his request. And then, just as the Prince was lifting Snow White onto his horse, the piece of apple, which unbeknown to anyone had been lodged in her throat, fell from her mouth, and she opened her eyes.

The wicked Queen could not believe it when her mirror said:—

"Oh Queen, although you are of beauty rare,
The Prince's bride is a thousand times more fair."

When she saw that Snow White was the Prince's bride, she choked with rage . . . and died.

Now Snow White had nothing to fear from the wicked Queen and she lived happily with her Prince, and visited the seven little dwarfs as often as she could.

The End

The Pied Piper of Hamelin

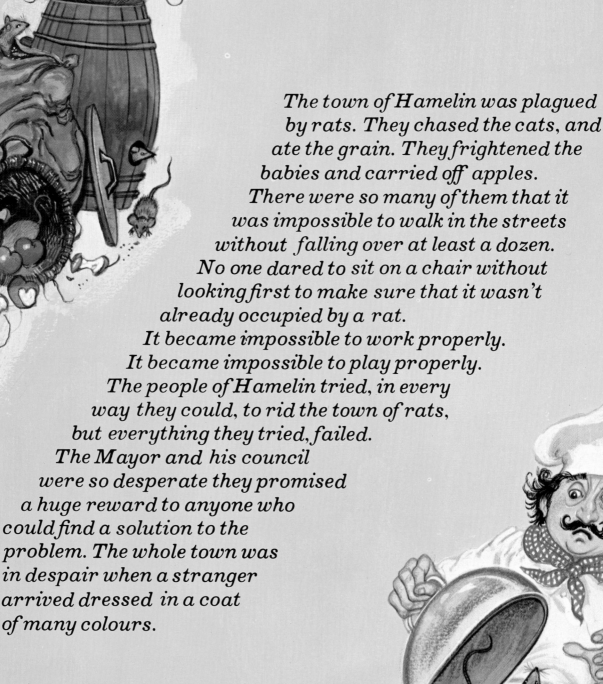

The town of Hamelin was plagued
by rats. They chased the cats, and
ate the grain. They frightened the
babies and carried off apples.
There were so many of them that it
was impossible to walk in the streets
without falling over at least a dozen.
No one dared to sit on a chair without
looking first to make sure that it wasn't
already occupied by a rat.
It became impossible to work properly.
It became impossible to play properly.
The people of Hamelin tried, in every
way they could, to rid the town of rats,
but everything they tried, failed.
The Mayor and his council
were so desperate they promised
a huge reward to anyone who
could find a solution to the
problem. The whole town was
in despair when a stranger
arrived dressed in a coat
of many colours.

"I have been told there is a reward for the man who rids this town of rats." he said.

"Anything . . . anything . . . if only you will help us," said the Mayor. The stranger in the pied coat walked to the middle of the town square and took a small pipe from his pocket. "What is he going to do?" whispered the townsfolk.

The stranger put the pipe to his lips and began to blow. As he blew a tune that grew gayer and gayer the rats began to creep from their holes to listen to him. When there were many gathered about his feet he began to walk through the town. Up streets and down streets he went and as he passed each door the rats left what they were doing and scampered after him. When he reached the town gate every rat in Hamelin was behind him. Still he strode on, across the meadow, towards the river.

"What is he going to do now?" asked the townsfolk.

When he reached the riverbank the piper in the pied coat stepped straight into the water.

It came to his knees.
The gay tune he was
piping grew sweeter and the rats
followed straight after him . . . and were all drowned.
The townsfolk shouted and cheered, but they were an ungrateful lot,
and as soon as the last rat was gone they hurried back to their
dinners and their games. No one even offered the piper a towel on
which to dry his feet.
The piper went to the Mayor and asked for his reward. The Mayor
faced him with a scowl. Now the rats were gone he saw no reason to
part with the money.
"Reward?" he said, "What reward? There is no reward.
Begone! Leave the town at once! You're not
wanted here!"
The piper did not say another word, but as
he walked through the streets of Hamelin to
the town gate, he began to blow another,
gayer, prettier tune on his pipe.
This time it wasn't the rats which ran from
the houses. It was the children.

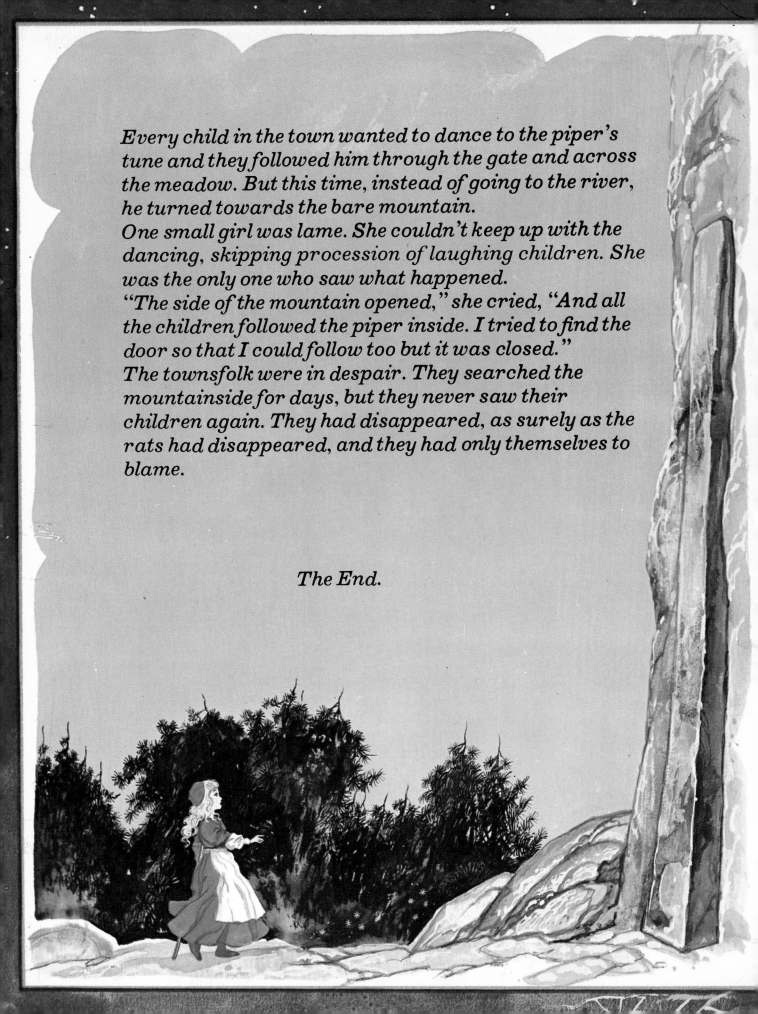

Every child in the town wanted to dance to the piper's tune and they followed him through the gate and across the meadow. But this time, instead of going to the river, he turned towards the bare mountain.

One small girl was lame. She couldn't keep up with the dancing, skipping procession of laughing children. She was the only one who saw what happened.

"The side of the mountain opened," she cried, "And all the children followed the piper inside. I tried to find the door so that I could follow too but it was closed."

The townsfolk were in despair. They searched the mountainside for days, but they never saw their children again. They had disappeared, as surely as the rats had disappeared, and they had only themselves to blame.

The End.

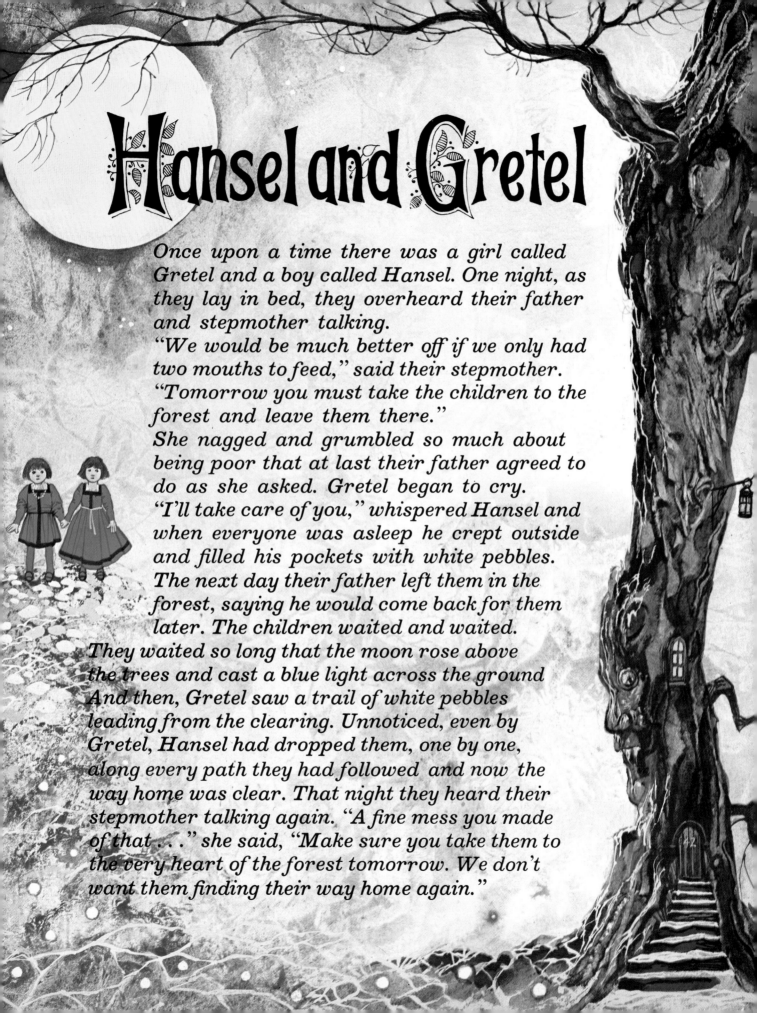

Hansel and Gretel

Once upon a time there was a girl called Gretel and a boy called Hansel. One night, as they lay in bed, they overheard their father and stepmother talking.

"We would be much better off if we only had two mouths to feed," said their stepmother. "Tomorrow you must take the children to the forest and leave them there."

She nagged and grumbled so much about being poor that at last their father agreed to do as she asked. Gretel began to cry.

"I'll take care of you," whispered Hansel and when everyone was asleep he crept outside and filled his pockets with white pebbles. The next day their father left them in the forest, saying he would come back for them later. The children waited and waited.

They waited so long that the moon rose above the trees and cast a blue light across the ground And then, Gretel saw a trail of white pebbles leading from the clearing. Unnoticed, even by Gretel, Hansel had dropped them, one by one, along every path they had followed and now the way home was clear. That night they heard their stepmother talking again. "A fine mess you made of that . . ." she said, "Make sure you take them to the very heart of the forest tomorrow. We don't want them finding their way home again."

"I'll gather some more pebbles," whispered Hansel, but when he went to fill his pockets he found the door of the cottage locked and bolted. The next day everything happened as it had done before, except that this time, instead of pebbles, Hansel left a trail of white bread crumbs. Alas, when the moon rose and the children looked eagerly for the crumbs to shine in the moonlight and show them the way home, they discovered there were no crumbs. The birds had eaten them. Now they were really lost.

They had been in the forest three days when they came upon a very strange house. Its walls were made of gingerbread. Its roof was covered with biscuit tiles. Its windows made of clear see-through toffee. The old woman who lived there invited them inside.

"How kind you are," said Gretel.

"How horrid she is," gasped Gretel when the witch, for the old woman was a witch, pushed Hansel into a cage and locked him in.

"Hee . . . hee . . ." said the witch, "Now little girl, you can feed your brother until he is fat enough to eat."

Every day the witch made Hansel eat pies and cakes and custard. She gave Gretel nothing but crusts and gravy.

"Don't worry," whispered Hansel. "I won't let her eat me." And every day, when the witch ordered him to put out his finger so that she could see how fat he was getting, he pushed a stick through the bars instead. The witch couldn't understand why he stayed so thin and bony. Then one morning she said crossly, "Get the oven ready girl . . . I'm tired of waiting."

Poor Gretel. The tears rolled down her cheeks as the witch made her stoke up the fire.

The oven got hotter and hotter. Poor, poor Hansel. What could she do to save him?

But it wasn't Hansel the witch had decided to cook. It was Gretel herself.

"Climb into the oven and test the temperature," she cackled. Hansel whispered a warning and Gretel realised just in time what the witch was about to do. The witch didn't get a chance to push her. Gretel pushed the witch instead.

"Let me out!" screamed the witch as Gretel slammed the oven door shut.

Gretel pretended not to hear. She let Hansel out of the cage and they ran into the wood without a backward glance.

They found a path which led them home. Their father was overjoyed to see them and they were overjoyed when he told them that their stepmother had gone. And so, once again, the three of them lived happily together.

The End.

Goldilocks and the Three Bears

Once there were three bears.
A father bear, a mother bear and
a baby bear.
One morning Mother Bear made
the porridge for breakfast as
usual. "The porridge is exceedingly
hot this morning," said Mother Bear.
"Let us go for a stroll in the wood while
it cools," said Father Bear.
There was someone else walking in the
wood that morning. A little girl, with
long golden hair, called Goldilocks. She
could smell the beautiful aroma of
porridge and she followed it, her nose
twitching, until she came to the open
window of the Bears' house. When she
saw the three bowls of steaming
porridge on the table they made her feel
so hungry she climbed in through the
window without so much as a 'please
may I?'
"I think I'll try some of that," she said.
She tried the porridge in the large
bowl first. It was so hot it burnt
her tongue.
"Ouch!" she said, and dropped
the spoon.

The porridge in the middle size bowl was far too sweet. "Ugh!" she said, and dropped that spoon too.

The porridge in the small bowl was just the way she liked it.

"Ooh lovely!" she said, and ate it all up.

When the small bowl was quite, quite empty she walked around the house opening cupboards, and looking at this, and looking at that, and trying everything she could see.

She sat on Father Bear's big chair.

"Oh no . . ." she said, "This is much too hard."

She sat on Mother Bear's middle size chair.

"Oh no . . ." she said, "This is much too soft."

She sat on Baby Bear's chair.

"Ooh lovely!" she said. "This is so comfortable."

But she wriggled and fidgeted about so much that one of the legs snapped in two and she fell to the floor.

She picked herself up and went into the bear's bedroom.

She tried Father Bear's big bed. "Oh no . . ." she said. "This is much too bumpy."

She tried Mother Bear's middle size bed. "Oh no . . ." she said, "This is much too squashy."

She tried Baby Bear's small bed. "Ooh lovely!" she said, "This is so comfortable."

And she fell fast asleep with her head on Baby Bear's pillow.

When the bears got home they could tell at once that someone had been inside the house.

"Who has been eating my porridge?" growled Father Bear.

"Who has been eating my porridge?" growled Mother Bear.

"And who has been eating my porridge, and finished it all up?" squeaked Baby Bear.

"Who has been sitting on my chair?" growled Father Bear.

"Who has been sitting on my chair?" growled Mother Bear.

"And who has been sitting on my chair, and broken it?" squeaked Baby Bear and he burst into tears.

"Who has been lying on my bed?" growled Father Bear.
"Who has been lying on my bed?" growled Mother Bear.
"Someone has been lying on my bed and she is still here." squeaked Baby Bear. "LOOK!"

Goldilocks opened her eyes and sat up. When she saw the three bears staring at her she jumped off the bed and out through the window so quickly the bears were taken by surprise.
The bears didn't bother to chase after her. She looked so frightened they knew she had learned her lesson and would never go uninvited into someone else's house again.
Instead, Mother Bear made some more porridge for Baby Bear. Father Bear mended his chair. And then they all sat down and had breakfast.

The End.

Beauty and the Beast

Once there was a rich merchant who had three daughters. Two were rather ugly, and always cross. The third was beautiful, and always kind. When the merchant lost his money and the family was forced to move from their grand house to a poky little cottage, the two cross and ugly sisters sat about all day and did nothing but grumble and complain. Beauty, as the youngest was called, looked after her father and her sisters. She cleaned the house, she cooked the food, made the beds and washed the dishes. She didn't complain at all.

One day the merchant came home with some good news. "I have been offered work in a distant town," he said. "When I return I would like to bring you all a gift. What shall it be?"

"A silk dress," said the two elder girls at once.

Beauty knew that her father hadn't enough money to buy gifts.

"I would like a rose . . ." she said, for she knew that a rose would cost nothing.

The merchant completed his business in the distant town some weeks later and began the journey home. On the way a storm blew up and somehow he missed a turning and lost his way. He climbed a tall tree in order to spy out the land and saw a distant castle. "Perhaps there will be someone there who can direct me," he thought and made his way towards it.

The castle door stood wide open. There was no one about but he had the curious feeling that he was expected. There were candles flickering in the candle sticks and logs blazing in the fireplace.

There was food upon the table, so he sat down and ate.

There was a bed prepared, so he lay down and slept.

In the morning he found fresh clean clothes in place of his old ones, and breakfast upon the table.

When he had eaten he went into the garden and picked a rose to take home to Beauty.

The morning quietness of the deserted castle was broken into a thousand splinters by an angry roar. He turned and came face to face with a creature which had the body of a man and the head of a beast. It was very angry indeed.

"I have made you welcome in my home, and now you abuse my hospitality by stealing from my garden . . . prepare to die." The merchant begged for his life. He explained that he had picked the rose for his daughter who was beautiful, and always kind.

At last the beast relented and said the merchant could go if he promised to send the first living thing he saw, when he returned home, to the castle in his place.

The merchant's dog was always the first to greet him when he had been away, so he gladly agreed and the beast let him go.

The merchant's joy at being home turned instantly to sorrow. His dog was inside the cottage lying asleep by the fire, and it was Beauty who ran to greet him.

She asked him why he looked so sad.

"I must say goodbye to you all," said the merchant. He couldn't send Beauty to the beast. He would return himself. But Beauty made him tell her what had happened, and in spite of his protests, she said she would go to the castle.

She shuddered when she saw the ugly beast.

"Do not be afraid." said the beast. "I will not harm you if you agree to stay here with me."

And so it was that Beauty's father went home sadly and Beauty stayed behind and tried not to be afraid.

Although the beast was so ugly he was kind and did everything he could to make Beauty happy.

One day he said, "Do you think me ugly?"

"Well . . . er . . . yes . . ." said Beauty.

"Will you marry me?"

"Oh no . . ." said Beauty, 'I cannot marry you."

Time passed and one day Beauty looked into her magic mirror and saw that her father was ill.

"Go home to him." said the beast. "But please return when he is well again."

Beauty's father soon recovered when he saw that Beauty was well and happy.

The days and the weeks went by and Beauty almost forgot about the beast.

And then, one night, she
dreamed that the beast was
dead. She woke from her
dream crying.
She dressed quickly and
using a ring which the beast
had given her she returned
to the castle.
At first she thought the beast
had gone, and then she saw him
lying by a fountain.
She gently splashed water on
his face to revive him.
"Dear beast . . ." she said,
"What does it matter that you
are so ugly . . . of course I will
marry you."
And then a wonderful thing
happened. The ugly beast turned
into a handsome prince, and
Beauty loved him as much as
she loved the ugly beast.
"I was bewitched . . ." said
the Prince, ". . . by a spell that
could only be broken when
someone loved me in spite of my
ugliness."
And that is how it came about
that the merchant gained a prince
as a son-in-law and Beauty
became a princess.

The End.

Once there was a Prince who wanted to marry a Princess. He travelled far and wide, for many months, searching for one. He met many girls who said they were Princesses, but somehow he could never be quite sure they were telling him the truth.

It was a very sad Prince who returned alone to the palace.

One dark night, not long after his return, there was a dreadful storm. It rained, and it thundered, and bright flashes of lightning lit up the sky. Everyone was saying how glad he was not to be outside, when there was a knock at the palace door. The King himself went to answer it.

A wet bedraggled girl stood shivering on the doorstep. "Come in, come in at once," he cried, "You must shelter here for the night."

When the girl was dry and warm again, and had eaten supper, she told them that she was a Princess. The Prince wished he could believe her, for of all the girls who said they were Princesses, this was the one he most wanted to believe.

Now the Prince's mother was very wise, and that night, without telling anyone what she was doing she re-made the girl's bed.

She put one tiny pea on the smooth wooden bed . . . and on top of the pea she put twenty soft mattresses . . . and on top of the mattresses, she put twenty, very soft, feather pillows. The girl had to climb almost to the ceiling before she could get into it!

Next morning the Queen asked her how well she had slept.

"I hardly slept at all," sighed the girl. "The bed was so lumpy, I tossed and turned and twisted all night."

As soon as she heard that, the Queen took the girl by the hand and led her to the Prince.

the Pea

"Only a real Princess could lie on so many soft mattresses and be unable to sleep because of one tiny pea," she said. And she explained to everyone what she had done.

The Prince was overjoyed, and he and the Princess were married, and of course they lived happily ever after. Princes and Princesses always do.

The End.

The Three Little Pigs

Once upon a time there were three little pigs who lived together in one house. As they grew bigger their house seemed to grow smaller, and one day they decided to build three separate houses.

The first little pig built himself a house of straw.

The second little pig built himself a house of sticks.

The third little pig built himself a house of bricks.

The house of bricks took much longer to build than the other two, but it was the strongest when it was finished.

Not long after the first little pig had moved into his house there was a knock at the door.

"Little pig, little pig let me come in," said the wily old wolf, thinking how nice it would be to have pig for dinner.

"No, no, by the hair of my chinny chin chin, I will not let you in," said the first little pig.

"Then I'll huff, and I'll puff, and I'll blow your house in," growled the wolf.

And that is exactly what he did. The straw house blew

away in the wind and the wolf
gobbled up the pig.

When the wolf saw the house
built of sticks, he licked his lips
and said:

"Little pig, little pig, let me
come in."

"No, no, by the hair of my
chinny chin chin, I will not let
you in," said the second little
pig.

"Then I'll huff, and I'll puff,
and I'll blow your house in,"
growled the wolf.

The house of sticks was almost
as easy to blow down as the
house of straw, and that was
the end of the second little pig.

The wolf knew there was a
third little pig about
somewhere and when he saw
the house of bricks he called
through the letter box.

"Let me in little pig."

"No, no, by the hair of my
chinny chin chin, I will not let
you in," said the third little
pig.

"Then I'll huff and I'll puff and
I'll blow your house in," said
the wolf.

And the wolf huffed and he

puffed, and he puffed and he huffed, until he was quite out of breath, and still the house of bricks stood firm and secure. It didn't even creak.

"I can see I'll have to be rather more clever to catch this little pig," said the wolf. "I'll have to lure him outside his house."

He told the little pig about a field he knew where the turnips were ready for digging, and arranged to meet him there next morning.

But the third little pig was

much cleverer than the wolf realised. He knew exactly what the wolf was up to. He had been to the field, dug up the turnips and was safely back indoors before the wolf had even woken up.

The wolf tried to keep his temper. He told the little pig about a tree he knew that was weighed down with juicy red apples.

"I'll meet you there in the morning," he said slyly.

The wolf wasn't going to be caught again and next day he

got up very early. When he reached the orchard the little pig was still in the tree picking apples.

"I'll throw you one," called the little pig, and he threw an apple so that it rolled into the long grass.

While the wolf was looking for it the little pig jumped from the tree and ran home. He was safely inside his brick house before the wolf realised he had been tricked.

By this time the wolf was getting very annoyed . . .

and hungry.

"I'll meet you at the fair tomorrow," he said.

The little pig did go to the fair next day. He bought himself a butter churn. He was on his way home when he caught sight of the wolf. As quick as a raindrop hiding in a puddle, he hid himself in the butter churn and began to roll down the hill. He rolled right over the wolf's foot and frightened him horribly. He was safely inside his brick house before the wolf stopped trembling.

When the wolf discovered who had been inside the butter churn he was very angry indeed. He was determined that the little pig should not escape again. He climbed on to the roof of the brick house and began to ease himself down the brick chimney.

The little pig was very frightened when he heard the wolf mumbling and grumbling inside his chimney, but he didn't panic. He built up the fire and set his biggest cooking pot on the flames.

The wolf slithered down the chimney and fell into the pot with an enormous splash and a very loud OUCH!!! And that, I am glad to say, was the end of the wolf.

The End.

The Brave Tin Soldier

Once, someone who was clever, made twenty-five tin soldiers from a single spoon. They were all painted in red and blue uniforms, and they all carried muskets over their shoulders. Except for the twenty-fifth, they were all exactly alike.

The twenty-fifth, and last, tin soldier was different simply because he was the last to be made. There hadn't been quite enough tin to finish him off and he had been left with one leg. Yet in spite of his handicap he was as brave, as smart, and as gallant as his companions, and fought many battles with them on the nursery floor.

Of all the other toys in the nursery, the little tin soldier most admired the dancer who stood in the doorway of the sparkling paste-board castle. She was as dainty and graceful as he was gallant and smart. She stood all the time on one leg, poised on the very tips of her toes, as dancers do. She held her other leg so high and straight behind her, that the little tin soldier, who had only seen her from the front, thought she had but one leg like himself.

He often thought how wonderful it would be if she would consent to become his wife. But she was so graceful and aloof, and he was so shy in spite of being so gallant, that he did not dare speak to her.

All he ever did was stand and stare.

The toy conjurer was jealous when he saw the tin soldier staring at the little dancer. "Stop staring" he said, "Or something will happen to you." But nothing could deter the little tin soldier. He didn't take his eyes off the dancer for a moment. He didn't even turn his head to reply.

The morning after the conjurer had issued his warning the tin soldier was standing on the nursery windowsill. Now whether the wind was responsible, or whether the conjurer had something to do with it or not, no one knows, but suddenly the window blew open and before anyone could stop him the little tin soldier fell three storeys to the street below and landed on his head.

The boy who owned the twenty-five tin soldiers went to look for him, but he was wedged between two paving stones and could not be found, and when it began to rain the boy gave up the search.

He was rescued from his predicament by two urchins

who were sailing paper boats
in the torrent that raced
along the gutter.
"I've found a captain for our
ship," said one. He stood the
little tin soldier in the bows
of the boat and pushed it off.
"How stiffly he stands," said
the other.
The paper boat bobbed along
the gutter with the tin soldier
standing stiffly to attention.
He knew no other way of
standing. Suddenly the boat
was swept into the darkness of
a drain. It was so dark the tin
soldier could see nothing with
his eyes at all but in his
imagination he saw the little
dancer and hoped that she
hadn't forgotten him.
The boat sped faster and
faster. It rolled and it rocked
and still the little soldier stood
firmly to attention. He was a
credit to his regiment.
They would have been proud
had they seen him. And then,
just as the boat came to the
end of the drain and it grew light,
the water fell, with a sudden gush,
into the canal.

The paper boat could hold out no longer. It began to fill with water. The little tin soldier sank lower and lower until only his head and the tip of his musket were above the water . . . and then they too disappeared.

He had almost reached the bottom of the canal, where he would have been lost for ever amongst the rubbish, when he was swallowed by a fish.

It had been dark inside the drain. It was twice as dark inside the fish. But even in the pitch black with no one to see him, the tin soldier still stood firmly to attention and kept his thoughts on the little dancer. He had almost given up hope of seeing her again when light suddenly burst in over his head like an exploding firework.

The fish had been caught and was being cleaned ready for cooking in the very house in which he had lived before his journey began. The maid recognised the little tin soldier and carried him to the nursery.

Everyone was anxious to see

the little soldier which had fallen from the window and ended up inside a fish but the little tin soldier himself only had eyes for the little dancer. She stood, aloof and graceful as ever, in front of the pasteboard castle.

And then, for no reason whatsoever, unless it was another trick of the jealous conjurer, one of the boys picked up the tin soldier and threw him into the fire.

The tin soldier felt the heat of the flames engulf him and knew then that the little dancer would never become his wife.

But just at the moment when the little tin soldier finally gave up hope, a door opened, a draught caught the dancer and she flew straight into the fire beside him. She disappeared in a flurry of sparks . . . and the little tin soldier melted right away.

The next morning when the maid was clearing the ashes from the fireplace she found a charred tinsel rose and the tiny tin heart of the brave little tin soldier.

The End.

The Elves and the Shoemaker

Once there was a shoemaker. He worked hard, but times were hard, and the day came when he was left with just enough leather to make one pair of shoes. He cut the pieces very carefully. One mistake, and there wouldn't have been enough leather to make even one pair. He put the pieces on the bench so that he could begin stitching them together the next morning and went to bed.

During the night, as he and his wife slept, something very mysterious happened.

"Wife! Come quickly!" he called when he went to start work next day.

On the bench, where the pieces of shoe leather had been, was now as fine a pair of finished shoes as they had ever seen.

"How could that have happened?" gasped his wife.

"We must have a friend," said the shoemaker. "And look how well they are made. I couldn't have made them better myself."

He sold the shoes that very morning, and for a very good price. Now he could buy enough leather to make two pairs of shoes. He cut the pieces and left them on his bench as he had done the previous night. When he came down to breakfast the following morning there were four finished shoes on the bench. And so it continued, night after night, after night. The more leather he was able to buy the more shoes he was able to cut. The more pieces he left on his bench, the more finished shoes he found in the morning. The more finished shoes he found, the more leather he was able to buy. It wasn't long before he began to grow rich for the shoes were so beautifully made everyone wanted to own a pair.

One evening, not long before Christmas, his wife said, "I wish we knew who was making the shoes so that we could thank them." The shoemaker wished the same thing himself, and they decided, there and then, that instead of going to bed that night they would stay up and keep watch.

At midnight the door opened and two elves came into the shop. They sat cross-legged on the bench and worked hard and diligently till all the pieces of leather had been sewn into shoes, and then they left, as quietly as they had arrived.

The shoemaker and his wife crept from their hiding place.

Naturally, they were astonished by what they had seen, but try as they would, they could think of no way of thanking the fairy-cobblers until the wife said.

"Did you notice how ragged their clothes were? I will make them each a new suit."

The shoemaker jumped to his feet and said,

"Did you notice that their feet were bare? I will make them both a pair of shoes."

The shoemaker and his wife were so pleased with their idea that they set to work the very next day. By Christmas Eve they had finished. The shoemaker had made four tiny shoes from the softest leather he could buy. His wife had made two pairs of tiny green breeches, two elegant green coats and two tiny frilled shirts, two pairs of white ribbed stockings which she had knitted on darning needles and two jaunty caps each trimmed with a mottled feather. They had taken as much care with their work as the elves did with theirs.

That night, instead of laying the pieces of shoe leather on the work bench they set out the new clothes. And then they hid and kept watch. At the stroke of midnight the two elves crept into the shop. When they saw the two sets of clothes they shouted with delight and threw down their shoemaking tools.

"We need make shoes no more." they sang, as they pulled on their white stockings. They danced from the shop dressed from tip to toe in their new clothes, as happy as any two elves could possibly be.

"How pleased they were," said the shoemaker as he hugged his wife.

"How elegant they looked," said the wife as she hugged the shoemaker.

The shoemaker and his wife never saw the elves again. But their luck had changed and the shoes the shoemaker made sold just as well as the shoes the elves had made, and he and his wife prospered and were happy ever after.

The End

The Frog Prince

A beautiful Princess was playing with her golden ball one day when she dropped it. It rolled to the edge of a deep clear pool and fell, with hardly a splash, to the bottom. She could see it lying on the white stones but she could not reach it, and soon her tears began to fall.

"Why are you crying?" asked a voice close by. The only creature the Princess could see was a slender green frog. She was so astonished to hear a frog speak that she answered immediately.

"My golden ball is lying at the bottom of the pool." she said sadly.

"If I bring it back to you," said the frog, "Will you let me sit upon your chair, share your food when you eat, and lie upon your bed when I am tired?"

"Anything, anything at all." promised the Princess. "If only you will bring my ball to me."

But alas, when the frog had dived to the bottom of the deep clear pool and retrieved the golden ball, the ungrateful Princess snatched it from him and ran laughing across the palace lawns.

She did not give the frog, or the promise she had made, another thought.

Next morning however, when she was skipping along one of the palace corridors, she met the slender green frog face to face, and she knew at once that he had come to claim his promise. She ran and hid behind her father, the King.

The King took her gently by the shoulder.

"You look very pale." he said, "Has something frightened you?"

The Princess told the King how the frog had returned her lost ball and of her promise to him, and how, at that very moment he was hopping along the palace corridor.

"Please make him go away father," she pleaded.

But the King said sternly, "A promise is a promise and must be kept. Invite the frog to our table."

Because she was a dutiful daughter the Princess did as she was told and the King and his five daughters sat down to breakfast. The frog hopped to the side of the Princess who had played with the golden ball.

"May I sit upon your chair?" he asked.

The Princess lifted him onto the polished wooden arm.

"May I share your food?" asked the frog.

The Princess lifted him to the side of her plate.

When the frog had eaten he said,
"I am tired, may I lie upon your bed?"
The Princess carried the frog to her bedroom, but she was so afraid
that the frog would hop onto the crisp white pillow upon which she lay
her own head, that she put him on a chair in the corner of the room
and hoped that that would do instead.
"I will tell your father you have not kept your promise," warned the
frog.
The Princess burst into a flood of tears. She picked up the frog and
threw him across the room to her bed.

"I have shared my chair with
you . . . I have shared my food
with you . . . must I really
share my bed with you?" she
sobbed.
And then, somehow, without
her really seeing just how it
happened, the slender green
frog turned into a handsome
young Prince who took her
hand and gently wiped away
her tears.

He had been bewitched and
because the Princess had
shared her chair, her food and
her bed with him, she had
broken the spell.

The Princess who played with
the golden ball, and the Prince
who had been a frog, were
married, of course, and they
lived happily ever after in a
land where promises were
always kept.

The End.

Sleeping Beauty

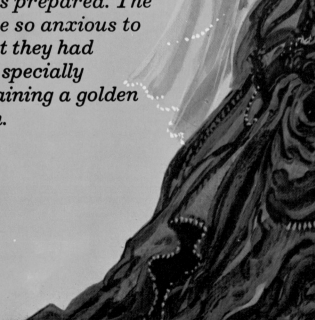

There was once a King and a Queen who longed for a child. After many years of waiting they at last had a daughter. Now at that time, any child who had a fairy as godmother was especially lucky. At the christening the fairy always gave the child a special gift. The King and Queen loved their little daughter so much they invited all seven fairies who lived in their kingdom to be godmothers.

The day of the christening came and a splendid banquet was prepared. The King and Queen were so anxious to please the fairies that they had seven golden caskets specially made, each one containing a golden knife, fork and spoon.

And then, something rather awful happened. As the King and his guests were taking their places at the banqueting table, an old fairy, whom no one had seen for years and years, arrived unexpectedly. The King immediately ordered another place to be set at the table, but alas, there were eight fairies and only seven golden caskets, and the old fairy had to eat with a silver knife, fork and spoon.

The old fairy was very angry. First she hadn't received an invitation and now she wasn't to have a golden casket. She thought she had been slighted on purpose, which wasn't the case at all, and she vowed she would have her revenge.

The time came for the fairies to bestow their gifts upon the baby Princess.

"She shall be as beautiful as a rose," said the first.

"She shall have the nature of an angel," said the second.

"She shall have the grace of a swan," said the third.

"She shall dance to perfection," said the fourth.

"She shall sing like a nightingale," said the fifth.
"She shall play the sweetest music," said the sixth.
No one could find the seventh fairy.
"She shall prick her finger on a spindle . . . and DIE!" cackled the old fairy.
Everyone present gasped, and turned pale. But before anyone could think what to say, or do, the seventh fairy reappeared. She had heard the old fairy mumbling and knew she was up to no good. She had waited until last to bestow her gift so that she could undo any harm done by the old fairy.
"The Princess will prick her finger . . ." she said, "But she will not die. Instead, she will sleep for a hundred years, and be woken by a prince."
The King was taking no chances. He ordered that all the spindles in his kingdom be destroyed. If there was no spindle for the Princess to prick her finger on, then there would be less reason to worry.

Sixteen years passed, and the
Princess grew more and more
beautiful. Then one day, when the
King and Queen were away, she
found an old tower. In the room
at the very top she found an old
woman spinning.

"What are you doing?" asked the
Princess. She had never seen a
spinning wheel before.

"I am spinning," said the old
woman, who for some reason had
never heard the King's order
regarding spindles.

"May I try?" asked the Princess,
and because neither she or the old
woman had heard of the fairy's
curse, she took the spindle when
the old woman handed it to her.
Alas, everything came about as
the fairy had predicted. The
Princess pricked her finger and
fell into a swoon from which she
did not wake.

There was so much wailing and
moaning in the castle that the
seventh fairy heard it. Now that
the Princess was alseep there was
something else she had to do.

She cast a spell so that everyone the Princess knew fell asleep and then she cast a spell round the castle itself so that thick thorns and brambles grew up around it and made it impossible for anyone to get anywhere near it.

A hundred years passed and many strange stories were told about the castle. Many tried to get into it, but no one succeeded. And then one day a King's son happened to pass that way. He asked about the castle and an old woodcutter told him a story he had heard from his own father about a princess and a magic spell.

The Prince was curious and decided to look for himself. He unbuckled his sword and prepared to hack through the thorns, but before he could touch them they seemed to melt away, and a path appeared which led to the castle gate.

The castle was very still. There wasn't a sound to be heard anywhere. He found the Princess on the couch where she had been gently laid a hundred years before. She looked so beautiful that he bent to kiss her.

And that was how the seventh fairy's prediction came true. The Prince's kiss woke the Princess, just as the fairy had said it would. And as the Princess woke, so everyone else in the castle woke, and life went on exactly from the point at which it had stopped a hundred years ago. It was as if nothing out of the ordinary had happened at all.

The Prince married the Sleeping Beauty who was now wide awake, and they lived happily ever after.

The End.

CHICKEN LICKEN

One morning, when Chicken Licken was sitting under an oak tree, an acorn fell upon his head.

"Oh dear." he gasped, "The sky is falling. I must run and tell the King."

On the way to the palace he met his friend Henny Penny.

"Where are you going?" asked Henny Penny.

"To tell the King the sky is falling," said Chicken Licken.

"Then I'll come with you," clucked Henny Penny.

Cocky Locky was scratching for grain.

"Where are you both going in such a hurry?" he asked.

"To tell the King the sky is falling," said Chicken Licken.

"Then I'll come with you," crowed Cocky Locky.

"Where are you all going?" asked Ducky Lucky, when she met them hurrying along a footpath.

"To tell the King the sky is falling," said Chicken Licken without stopping.

"Then I'll come with you," quacked Ducky Lucky.

"Where are you all going?" called Drakey Lakey from the pond.

"To tell the King the sky is falling," said Chicken Licken.

"Then I'll come with you," said Drakey Lakey shaking the water from his webbed feet.

Goosey Loosey was as anxious as everyone else to help tell the King the bad news.

"I'll come with you," she hissed as she stretched her long white neck.

"And I'll come too . . . too . . . too . . ." gobbled Turkey Lurkey who didn't like to be left out of anything.

Foxy Loxy was lurking behind a bush.

"Where are you all going in such a hurry?" he asked slyly.

"To tell the King the sky is falling," said Chicken Licken.

"Then you had better follow me." said Foxy Loxy. "I know of a short cut."

And he led Chicken Licken, Henny Penny, Cocky Locky, Ducky Lucky, Drakey Lakey, Goosey Loosey and Turkey Lurkey through the bushes to his den, where his wife and five hungry children were waiting.

And that, I am sorry to say, was the end of Chicken Licken, Henny Penny, Cocky Locky, Ducky Lucky, Drakey Lakey, Goosey Loosey and Turkey Lurkey, for the fox family had them for dinner, and the King never did find out that a piece of the sky had fallen on Chicken Licken's head.

The End.

CINDERELLA

There was once a girl called Cinderella. She lived with her father and her step-sisters in a huge house. Cinderella was beautiful. Her step-sisters were ugly. Cinderella was kind and gentle. Her step-sisters were unkind and spiteful. They spent their time trying to make themselves look pretty and they made sure Cinderella spent her time cleaning and washing and scrubbing so that no one would notice she was more beautiful than they. One morning, when Cinderella was scrubbing floors, there was a great commotion.

"Look what we've got," cried the ugly sisters, dancing round and round the kitchen and leaving a pattern of big muddy footmarks all over the newly washed floor. They dangled a gilt-edged card under Cinderella's nose. "We have got an invitation to the King's ball. We are going to meet the Prince. I dare say he will want to marry one of us."

"Oh please . . . may I go the ball?" asked Cinderella. The ugly sisters hooted with laughter.

"You . . . go to the ball . . . how silly you are. You haven't a thing to wear." Which was perfectly true. Poor Cinderella only had a brown ragged dress and a sackcloth apron. "And besides, we will need you to help us get ready."

The ugly sisters had a wardrobe full of beautiful ball gowns and trunks full of elaborate wigs. They had boxes, and boxes, of sweet smelling powder. They had countless bottles of sweet smelling lotions. It took them hours and hours to get ready to go anywhere, let alone somewhere as important as the King's ball. On the night of the ball they led poor Cinderella a merry dance.

"Fetch that . . . alter this . . . press that . . . tie this . . . find that . . . do it this way . . . undo it . . . do it up . . . stop pulling . . . pull it tighter . . ."

Poor Cinderella felt quite dizzy by the time they were both powdered and bewigged and fastened into their ball gowns.

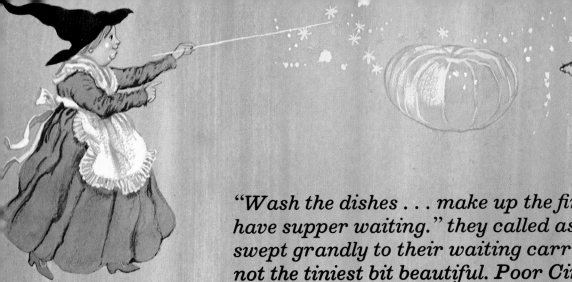

"Wash the dishes . . . make up the fire . . .
have supper waiting." they called as they
swept grandly to their waiting carriage looking
not the tiniest bit beautiful. Poor Cinderella.
She did the chores then sat beside the fire and
wept. She did so want to go to the ball.

Suddenly there was a flash of light. She thought at first it was a
burst of sparks from the fire and then she saw a strange little
woman wearing a pointed hat and carrying a wand of dancing
stars.

"Do not be afraid," she said, "I am your fairy Godmother. You
shall go to the ball."

"But I have no dress to wear," said Cinderella sadly. "I cannot
go to the ball wearing rags."

"You are not wearing rags now," said the fairy. She had touched
Cinderella's tattered brown dress with her wand. She had
changed it into a beautiful ball gown and had put glass slippers
on Cinderella's bare feet.

The fairy called for a pumpkin. She touched that with her wand
and turned it into a coach. She turned eight white mice into eight
white horses. Six green lizards into six liveried footmen.

A rat into a coachman.

"You must be home by midnight," said the fairy as Cinderella stepped into the coach. "My magic stops at midnight and your ball gown will become rags again."

Cinderella danced with the King's son all evening. He couldn't take his eyes off her. He thought her the most beautiful girl he had ever seen. Cinderella had never been so happy in her life. She was so happy she forgot time was ticking past and it wasn't until the clock began to strike twelve that she remembered the fairy's warning.

"Wait . . ." cried the Prince, as she slipped from his arms, "You haven't told me your name . . ."

There was no time to stop. Cinderella ran from the ballroom without a backward glance.

Seven . . . eight . . . nine . . . she lost a slipper as she ran down the palace steps. She did not dare stop to pick it up . . .

Ten . . . eleven . . . on the twelfth stroke her beautiful ball gown became rags and her coach turned back into a pumpkin. She ran home with her feet bare and with the mice, the rat and the lizards scurrying behind her.

But one thing hadn't changed and that was the glass slipper which lay on the palace steps. It was the Prince himself who found it. He recognised it at once.

"I will marry the girl who can wear this slipper," he said, "No matter who she is."

He sent messengers across the land with orders that every girl in the kingdom was to try the slipper. Eventually they came to the house where Cinderella and her step-sisters lived. The ugly sisters were so excited. They snatched the glass slipper from the messenger before he could say a word.

"Look . . . it fits me . . ." said the eldest.

"But your heel is hanging out," said the messenger.

"It fits me . . . it fits me . . ." said the youngest.

"But your toes are bent double," said the messenger, and then he asked, "Is there anyone else who would like to try the slipper?"

Before Cinderella could answer one of the ugly sisters clapped a hand over her mouth.

"She's only a serving maid . . . the slipper won't fit her."

But the messenger had his orders. Of course, the slipper fitted Cinderella perfectly. As she slipped her foot into it her fairy godmother appeared with her magic wand in one hand and the second glass slipper in the other.

"Cinderella shall marry the Prince," she said, and with a touch of her wand she changed Cinderella's rags into the beautiful gown she had worn at the ball.

"It was you . . . it was you who stole the Prince from us . . ."
shouted the ugly sisters, their eyes nearly popping out of their
heads. "It's not fair . . . it's not fair . . ." They stamped their feet
and pouted and sulked.
No one took any notice of them at all. There was a royal wedding
to plan and that was far more important.

The End.